Sawn-off Tales

Sawn-off
Tales

DAVID GAFFNEY

SALT

CAMBRIDGE

PUBLISHED BY SALT PUBLISHING
PO Box 937, Great Wilbraham PDO, Cambridge CB1 5JX
United Kingdom

© David Gaffney, 2006

The right of David Gaffney to be identified as the
author of this work has been asserted by him in accordance
with Section 77 of the Copyright, Designs and Patents Act 1988.

First published 2006
Reprinted 2006, 2007

Printed in Great Britain by the MPG Books Group, Bodmin and King's Lynn

Typeset in Berthold Caslon 12/18

ACKNOWLEDGEMENTS

The author would like to thank the editors of the following
publications where some of these stories first appeared: *Ambit,
The Illustrated Ape, The Mix, Opium, The Phone Book* and *Transmission.*

ISBN-13 978 1 84471 282 3 hardback
ISBN-10 1 84471 282 6 hardback

ISBN-13 978 1 84471 292 2 paperback
ISBN-10 1 84471 292 3 paperback

5 7 9 8 6 4

for Susan

Contents

Your Name in Weetos

I WAS A stacker, working nights. I had been incubating a desire for Mildred for a long time and that night she was nearby, on chillers, wearing plastic gloves and a paper hat. I was on cereals, yard after yard of gaudy motifs repeating like a nagging one-note riff. I shuffled the boxes around and called her over.

She laughed. 'My name in Weetos. Thanks, mate.' Then she went to the deli and daubed *William* onto the sneeze shield with squeezy-cheese. I was going to say something else when the shift super arrived and broke us up. We never spoke again. At the end of the summer she went to university and I stayed on stacking. Stacking suited me. You filled the shelves, the stuff got sold, you filled them up again. There were other female stackers, but I wasn't interested. To my mind, a moment can be worth a whole relationship.

The Lost Language of Hairgrips

THE TINY THINGS she had. The tweezers, the eyelash curlers, the cuticle pushers, all of them so small, so brittle. That's what I miss most about Joanna. The little things. Not the little things she did, or the little things she said; the actual little physical things she owned.

Without Joanna's little things littering the place, everything looked giant. Overstuffed chairs, hulking shampoo bottles, breeze block soap. I possessed nothing small enough to be mislaid and this thought disturbed me, made me feel feline and uneasy.

One night I was rubbing one of Joanna's hairgrips against the cheese grater, sending orange plastic slivers spinning into my soup, when I realised this obsession was completely wrong. What I needed were some little things of my own.

I discovered the answer in the aisles of the DIY store. Here were a billion little things for men to own and cherish; curious devices like the discarded tools of a lost civilisation. I filled my trolley and wheeled it to the checkout, but before I'd even paid I met Pat. Pat had just one item in her trolley – a giant architectural plant – and, following my eyes, she told me that there was nothing she hated more than little things. When her last fellah brought home a pathetic little plastic man to wave at his toy locomotives, it was the final straw.

'There's something sinister,' Pat explained to me in the car, 'about little things. I worry that they will divide and multiply in the night, creep inside me, and possess me. You know where you are with a big thing. A big thing would never do that.'

I fell in love with Pat. Everything about her was big. Her house had huge bay windows like a comforting bosom into which I sank each night. I forgot completely about the little things. Think big, Pat said, and I did.

Last to Know

H E SHOWED ME the back of my head in a mirror and I nodded. '£6.50 then,' he said, and pressed the foot pedal. The hydraulics sighed as I sank to the floor.

'I normally pay five.'

He indicated the price list. 'It's been £6.50 for a while.'

'Yes, but . . .'

What had happened? I was regular. Only new customers paid full. It was never spoken of, but that was the system. The barber could tell that someone else had cut it; the blending between the longer and shorter sections was poorly executed.

'Look me in the eye,' he said, 'and tell me you haven't been to anyone else.'

'I haven't been to another barbers in years.'

The barber sucked in his lower lip. 'So we're talking home clippers.'

'Yes,' I said, and felt my cheeks redden in shame.

'OK. Call it £5.50. I know you won't do it again.'

Flying Lessons with Gary Numan

HIS FACE WAS scratched, his clothes dishevelled, but he looked alright, not like he would lunge at you with a sharpened toothbrush or anything. He was going to watch Man City training – it was free and it passed a morning – and all he needed was the bus fare, so I gave him £1.40. He told me about his son, well his stepson really, who had got pally with Gary Numan, the singer. But Mr Numan didn't sing anymore, he flew planes.

This relationship infuriated my new friend – did I know what music was all about? The Moody Blues were what music was all about. But the year before, when the hostel got him a free ticket to see his heroes at the Apollo, he leapt onto his seat, shouted, 'Justin, Justin', and a huge fuck-off bouncer chucked him out. 'It's all,' he spat onto the road, 'synthesisers now.'

Intimate Zone

I COULDN'T BELIEVE it. He pushed through the door and squeezed himself onto the same seat. Right next to me, you know, touching. I told him I wouldn't be long but he starts right in with this stuff about different cultures. 'We English,' he says, 'we worry too much about personal space. I've just landed back from Spain and they have a completely different attitude. You are sitting on a deserted beach and another group of Spaniards appear? They set up right next to you. On an underground train alone? The next Spaniard will plonk down on the same seat. It's a liberating attitude. We English are too distrustful.'

There was nothing I could do to get rid of him. So I climbed off, yanked up my jeans and flushed. The cold water splashed up onto his bare skin and he just sat there looking up at me.

Happy Place

HE HATED GROCERY shopping, hated the time it took. But he came up with a method. People bought the same things, more or less. So he would look for someone of his type, sneak up behind them and roll their fully-laden trolley off to the checkout.

It made life interesting. Often there were things he would never have bought; once there was a fat orange pumpkin.

But today he was in trouble. He had been stealing mostly from women because he liked the sense of order to their selections, but his victim had spied him and was stomping over. There were women's products in the cart, so it was going to be difficult. He decided to pretend he knew her.

'Darling, I'll just get eggs.'

'We've got eggs,' the woman chirped. 'Listen, do you want to go out to the car? You look stressed. You can listen to your tape.'

Where We Left Off

At 12.30 EVERY weekday he visited HMV and stood in the same place for exactly four minutes. Because that's where he last saw her, eleven years, three months and two days ago. The F section of rock and pop. Blue denim jacket, red jumper, red bag.

He hadn't seen her since. So today, when she appeared in different clothes and a much-altered hairstyle, he was at first unsure if it was her.

But it was. He knew exactly what he was going to say, had rehearsed it every day in front of a mirror, but suddenly his mouth was dry and the words tumbled out as an incoherent squawk. She just stared at him then stalked out of the shop.

He would continue his mission. The faint expression of disdain that had crossed her face all those years ago when she came across that CD by The Fall was unforgivable.

You Know, Quiet

THE ROOM HE was given had seven wardrobes. Seven. At night the wardrobes oppressed him. Dark brooding figures shuffling closer to his bed, faces glowering out from the whorls of polished grain. The landlord wouldn't let him get rid of them. They were classic. Solid. So he had to think of a way to use them. The TV fitted into one, hi-fi in another, cooking equipment in a third, and various bits and bobs in the rest. But he couldn't think of anything to do with the last one. Then one night he dragged his duvet into it and had the best night's sleep ever.

He decided to stay in the wardrobe. He would move in a radio, and would eat there too. Eventually he would get six more people to live in the other wardrobes. Because he was the last person to keep himself to himself.

Uchafu

I watched her face, listening closely, just like it said in the book. But loud laughter from the kitchen made it difficult to concentrate.

'Your bill,' the waiter said through a leery grin, 'Mr Dirty Bastard.'

I looked at him.

'The word on your T-shirt.'

The T-Shirt was from a trendy city centre shop—be casual, be modern, the book said. I'd assumed the inscription on the back was just a random collection of letters.

'*Uchafu.* It's Swahili. Means "dirty bastard",' the waiter chuckled, 'or literally, "he who pimps for a slave owner".'

On the way back I made light of it. 'Somewhere in Africa, there's a T-shirt with "knobhead" on the back.' But she didn't laugh. Do not enter the next phase unless the mood is right, the book said, so I took her straight home. She would talk to the agency about me, I knew it.

What You Know
is There

I F HE WAS serious about finding someone to share his life he should take up some pastime.

'And one,' his therapist added sternly, 'that a woman might share,' referring, unfairly he thought, to his collection of electric and manual drills.

The card was in Chorlton post-office. A new therapy for a new age. Registered practitioner.

'It's a mixture of dance and acupuncture,' the lady on the phone told him. 'We call it dance-upuncture. The tutor is very very intelligent, very very sensitive, very in the moment, very evolved; more than her linear years.'

'Sounds like a laug,' he said. 'Book me in.'

The police made him draw a picture. The

girl poised delicately in an arabesque, the trip on the stool, the collision, the fall, the blood. But he couldn't draw the needles. Always draw what you see, the police artist kept saying. Not what you know is there.

Pets

THEY HAD PICKED up the guinea pigs from the Bitch-on-Wheels and were on their way back when the snow started to really hammer down. Ray's dad said that the road – a single tracker – would definitely get clogged-up, so he stopped and swung the car on to what turned out to be a frozen pond. There was a loud crack and they tilted forward. Water gushed in through the front and under the doors.

His dad shouted, 'Get on to the roof! Climb out through the window – I'll go for help!'

The car lurched and swayed under him and Ray watched his dad's back running back to the Bitch-on-Wheels. He closed his eyes against the stabbing cold.

The icy water at his ears roused him and

there was his dad and the Bitch-on-Wheels –
kissing. Ray couldn't understand why they
weren't running for help.

Killer Lines

I F THAT'S A triangle, my arse is a dodeca-hedron. Ray had lots of lines like that, killer lines, lines he appeared to have invented on the spot but had really spent ages preparing. That's why his friends considered him hilarious, going so far as to say he could make it as a stand-up. He would wait months for the right circumstances to use a killer line. On national Take-Your-Kids-To-Work-Day, a killer line came into his head involving a famous secure hospital for paedophiles. But the name of the institution wouldn't come, so he waited a year till the day came round again.

But today it fell apart. Marketing-Alison waved a tea bag saying what shape is this, and he was about to deliver when Sales-Mark burst in with a pyramid quip. Ray had a competitor.

But worse, the undetonated killer line was still inside him—what damage could it do?

Click

PHILLIP READ THE note again. "Bang, bang you're dead". The building was eerily silent. The other tenants never seemed to make any sounds. If they were seabirds, and their tiny rooms cliff ledges, they would shriek out to let each other know they were there. Even confined prisoners communicated by beating tattoos on the walls and pipes. In films, anyway. He imagined the outer wall stripped away, its miserable inhabitants exposed, crouched alone in the same positions, like waxworks.

He lit a fag, sucked it in and looked out of the window, down into a dark yard. Then he folded the note and went out into the hall. The doorknob, letterbox and spyhole on his neighbour's door formed an inscrutable face. He

pushed the note inside. In a few moments the
door would be flung open – it usually was – and
when that happened Phillip would be ready.

Into the World

STOP. REWIND. PLAY. A camera nosing through purple velour curtains. A mucky window, the rhomboid prints of a miskicked football and the crushed corpse of a fly clinging to the glass with congealed gut. A hand print showed where the peeper had steadied herself. A line of digits whirred away. Then the focus lengthened and Derek saw his own car creep up his own drive and stop. Derek, dressed in overalls, emerged, hobbled round to the boot, and dipped in and dragged out his tool bag. He hauled out another and bundled them into the house.

'You sponging bastard,' a voice close to the camera hissed. 'Got you!'

Lines of static forked across, the speaker whooshed.

The video came with a letter. "Benefit Integrity Project. Claim Suspended". Derek looked out of the window at his mother's house, at the purple velour curtains, the curtains she had chosen before he left.

Heavy Java Guy

EARN THE JARGON and you can get any job. 'Quick question, out of the gate,' the technogeek says. 'What have you done Unix-wise? It all seems to be,' he glanced down at my CV, 'shell scripting, some stuff on the thread management side. I'm wondering how I match you up with our environment. Aren't you the heavy Java guy, done a lot of clusters?'

I saluted. 'That's me.'

'Thing is, I don't hear anyone screaming "I know Solaris down to the bones".'

'Call me X-Ray.'

He slumped back and spread his arms. 'Come to me, baby.'

But I didn't take it. The next day I had an interview for a music therapy job and they have gorgeous language; string-washes, brass-stabs, sobbing bass. I never take the jobs, it's the words I like, the sound of them nudging against each other, and the gawping faces of a panel hungry to listen.

She's Really Alt-Country

I SPOTTED HER at The Be Good Tanyas, moving her head to the music in a dreamy circling motion as if she were drawing a figure of eight in the air with her nose.

When I got home I wrote her a song, all about a country singer who hitches up with a fifteen-year-old girl. It goes

> *We called it love*
> *The Judge called it assault*
> *But they used to call it Country*
> *And now they call it Alt*

and after a Jesse Mallin gig, I handed her the cassette.

For a moment we were both holding the same piece of plastic, then I remembered that on the tape you could make out my mother bawling, 'Geordie, your Pop-Tarts are cremated,' and me saying, 'Shut up, you old bag,' in a pathetic hissy whisper.

So I snatched it back and mumbled that I'd see her at Calexico next week.

Smells Like

GORDON'S LIP CURLED into a sneer when he saw me applying roll-on deodorant. 'What you putting that stuff on for?'

'There's a lot of attractive women at our place,' I explained. 'I like to smell nice.'

'You have no idea, mate,' Gordon said. 'Those pretty whiffs won't get their engines running. Women are turned on by the real smell of a man. Sour sweat, rotting skin cells. It's a mainline into the bits of the brain that control desire.' He put his hands behind his head and looked at the ceiling. 'I use no artificial scents of any kind and I have never – except for that time in Asda – been turned down by a reasonable woman.'

So I haven't used any fragrances for two

weeks now and I think it's making a difference. Women keep asking me if I live alone, and that's always a good sign.

Some Call it Loungecore

I CALL IT shite. A-plinking and a-plonking, a-twanging and a-trilling, kitsch Oxfam vinyl with titles like *Hammond Interlude*, *Moog TV Themes* and *Test Card Classics*, it's all Roger buys. And if our mates come round (like we have any now) it's *Beatles Hawaiian Style* or *Sinatra's Pan Pipe Moods* and him sitting with a big grin on his face stroking his chin.

Lounge music won't do any lasting harm, the doctor assured me, though wearing a permanent ironic smile doesn't help when you're stopped for speeding. But Roger's manager was worried. Sales were down and he blamed the easy-listening. 'That Radio 2 mush,' he said, 'is chewing off your balls,' and he forced on him some poodle-rock compilation.

'Oh my fucking God,' Roger said to me. *'Music to Drive By*. What does that even mean?' and fed the tape into the waste disposal, meaning we had to call the engineer.

Special Interest

'EXCUSE ME,' HE said. It was the bloke who'd been creeping around behind me in Woolworths. He had haunted muddy eyes and his breath reeked of curry and tic tacs.

'I was wondering, did you pay for those seeds?'

He was right of course. Assorted Summer Blooms, palmed deftly into my secret pocket. But this guy didn't look like security.

'What seeds?'

His eyes darted about. 'Can we go for coffee?'

His thumb stroked my finger where it rested against my Latte. I didn't move it away.

'I have a thing,' he said, 'for people like you.'

I felt myself redden. 'Like me?'

He gripped my finger in his hand. 'Women who steal.'

I pulled my hand away. 'So I'm just another?'

'You're special. I bet you don't even have a garden for those seeds.'

'One o'clock, B&Q,' I called after him. 'Nails and fixings.'

We Are the Robots

SHE WAS THE third girlfriend to ditch me this year. 'We went to this club,' I told Gary, 'and at the end of the night she'd completely changed. She was distant, hostile.'

He looked at me over the rim of his spectacles. 'Did you dance?'

'Well,' I poked at a beer mat, 'at one point I did throw a few shapes.'

He tilted his head towards me. 'Did you do the robotics?'

'Definitely not.'

'What was the music?'

'Eighties techno.'

Gary removed his spectacles and rubbed his eyes. 'How many times have we been through this – you hear the music, you do the robotics.'

He picked up his coat. 'No woman will stand for it.'

Later I was on the floor. A Moog bass line squelched, a metallic snare ripped the air, I was part of a machine, a valve in the heart of a bleeping gnashing metal beast.

Little Jan

I WAS THE only Janet in the office until she arrived but there was no problem until one day I asked Harriet for the long stapler and she said she'd given it to Little Jan.

Little Jan. She wasn't particularly little and I'm not especially big. I didn't want to be known as Big Jan, like some bull dyke prisoner. Harriet tried to reassure me; the new Janet was Little Jan, but I would always be Jan. But they might as well write fat cow on my forehead for all the difference that made. So-called Little Jan is a 12 at least, and not TopShop, more like Marks.

So whilst recovering the long stapler I told Jan all about fast-track promotion in this place, the people to influence, and how to do it.

Now I'm still Jan but she's known as Stock-room Jan and she's off long-term with stress.

A Good System

I WAS WORKING in Kendal's café then. You had to assume the woman he came in with was his wife. They were given, as everyone was, a long metal stand with the order number on it. It's a good system, we should have it here. Their little boy sat holding it.

When you're a waitress you don't miss a thing. So I immediately saw his eyes meet the eyes of a woman in a black furry coat. Then I heard the loud rasp as she slid her chair back and the tick tick of her heels crossing the room. The man looked up at her – he was terrified, frozen. Then she punched him in the face and returned to her friend.

I remember the silence in the room and the

little boy holding the order number higher and
higher like it was some sort of distress signal.

We Like it Here

THE SORTING HALL was said to be a special department where people with no useful function were sent. No-one knew if it really existed. One lunchtime he scoured Industry House, from the rooftop to the basement, looking for it. He saw suited executives nibbling biscuits, girls tapping at computers, men at drawing boards and, in a room marked *Training*, a group building a structure with toilet-roll holders. But there was no trace of the sorting hall.

Back at his desk they had already brought the afternoon's bins. He looked forward to examining the contents as there was always something exciting. He began to classify, measure and catalogue. A tissue, which he placed in a twizzle bag and labelled. A crumpled A4 sheet to be smoothed out and placed in a file. A crisp packet.

He enjoyed his job. He would leave Industry House altogether if anything ever changed.

No Turning

THIS STREET IS a dead-end and people are always using our drive to turn round when they're lost and it does my dad's head in. This family reversed up, but instead of screeching off again, they sat for ages arguing over the map. So my dad went out. The bushy-haired driver smiled. 'We're looking for the ferry.'

We never went to the ferry, we never went anywhere.

'Can't you read?' my dad moaned, pointing to his slapped-up NO TURNING sign.

The man shrugged.

But he was surprised when my dad screamed down the road in mum's car to stop in a cloud of dust and block them in.

We kept them for two hours. The girl was my age and she hated these holidays, driving for miles in a steaming car. I let her have a go of my Gameboy. I'm glad my dad kidnapped them; I hope he does it again.

Last Chance to Turn Around

SHE'D BEEN COMING every week. Late forties, right age for the hey-day, had some of the moves as well, a slide and a nifty shuffle on the backbeat. She was normally with a bloke, but she was alone tonight and after my set she beckoned me over, handed me a scratched 45 and said, ' I've been meaning to return it.' It was Tobi Legend, *Time Will Pass You By*.

'You gave it to me.'

'Me?'

'Twisted Wheel, 1974.'

Something about the way she sipped her wine struck a chord and I suddenly remembered her.

'I'll never forget that night,' she said. 'It wasn't a fair exchange.'

I stared into the hole in the centre of the disc as if it was a time-tunnel, sucking me down thirty swirling years. I had nothing to give her back. We sat and soaked in the songs till the landlord chucked us out.

Mask

ER NOSE HAD a cute little ridge and he stroked it with his thumb. 'I think Sharon suspects,' he said.

She looked into his eyes. Tips of her red hair clung to his face with static. 'As long as we're careful, Richard.'

Driving back, Richard couldn't stop thinking about her. The car was bathed in her perfume, Hugo Boss surrounded him like a Ready brek halo. That's when he panicked. He sniffed his fingers and rubbed them on the seat, but the smell wouldn't shift. What could he do? Sharon would be onto him like a hyena. His eyes fell on a half-eaten cheese baguette sweating on the dash. He stopped the car on a dark bridge, removed his shirt and, remembering something about pulse points, applied slimy sandwich filling to his wrists, throat and under his arms. He relaxed and shoved his seat into recline. Below him chains of crimson tail-lights danced and he felt he was floating over a fairy grotto.

The Kids Are Alright

WHEN I HEARD about the boy whose parents dressed him as a girl till the age of twelve I thought, lucky kid. My parents dressed me till I was thirteen as popular crooner Perry Como. They even encouraged me to carry, but not smoke, a beautiful briar wood pipe and I would stab the air with its stem to emphasis a point and suck on it when deep in thought. Yet I wasn't unhappy; it was normal. My cousin had it much worse, as Max Bygraves.

One day I was house-training the dog. The sleeve to *Swing Out Perry* was on the floor and before I could stop him, Engelbert squatted and squeezed a neat little turd right in the middle of Perry's polished inane features.

The next day my mother let me have my

fringe cut like Dave Hill out of Slade. Kids have to be allowed to express themselves.

Tasting Notes

ERE SHE COMES, Rentaghost Girl. Every month it's the same. She lifts it, eyes it, sniffs and slurps, then scribbles some twaddle about eighties cop shows, psychedelic garage bands, and Rentaghost. To her, every wine tastes like seventies kids' sitcom, Rentaghost.

This one was a pinot noir with no *grand cru* status, but a nice jagged aftertaste, owing to the vine's roots struggling deep through limestone rock. I jumped in first. 'I get Harvey Kietel, late James Ellroy and a John Zorn sax solo.'

Rentaghost Girl flapped her notebook. 'I'm sorry,' she said. 'I have a cold tonight and everything tastes like Pardon My Genie, but I do think you might have this wrong. Open your mouth.' I did, and she dipped a finger into

the wine and rubbed it over my tongue, gums,
lips and around the insides of my cheeks.
'Now,' she said, 'can you taste the seventies?'

Wednesday Night's Alright for Fighting

'ACCOUNTANCY'S NOT AS boring as everyone thinks. There's lots of testosterone. They shout, actually shout at each other, and someone once got punched. Physical violence, that's accountancy nowadays. So it was always a tough week for him, I knew that, and normally we'd only meet at weekends, but I rang him one Wednesday and said, "Do you want come over?"—he was only down the road in Didsbury—and he says no, he's got early meetings, he can't drink or anything, and I said not a drink, just come and see me—you know, see me. And he says, "oh," goes quiet, then says, "I don't do that during the week, normally." Can you imagine? Doesn't do it during the week? The bloke I'm with now goes like a ferret.'

'What's his job?'

'Sales. It's all about presentation skills, apparently.'

Contact Time

I SEE MY kid every weekend, but it always ends in tears. When I told him about the man with one ear who went into a pub, he didn't laugh, he cried. What happened to his ear? Was he the same man who bought the slippers off the bloke with no legs? Was the pub the one with the microwave where they put the poor duck to make it into Bill Withers?

So I gave him maths instead. I told him about a farmer with three lengths of rope and we worked out the average length, then calculated a 20% reduction on a shirt in last year's style. But this troubled him too. What was last year's style? And was it bought by the farmer with the rope showing his ignorance of fashion?

Now we play 'snap'. If we stay away from the picture cards, it's fine.

Enclosures

I SAW HIM every day, sucking on a tube of Superstrength or curled up like a foetus in his tattered sleeping bag and I thought about our armadillo munching his vegetables, our pumas tearing into slabs of glistening steak, our zebras in their warm straw beds and I called him over and said come with me.

I placed him in an empty orang-utan unit and told him to stay out of sight during opening times. I put two solvent abusers in with the giraffes and the muttering shopping-trolley woman onto gibbon island.

But the shopping-trolley woman kept showing her bottom to school children and the boss called me in. He was pleased with my intervention, but could the new guests be given educational classes like art, music and dance so that

the public could watch? This would be the
zoo finally putting something back into the
community.

New Best Friend

FTER THE CONSULTANT left, Tim called us into his office and handed round a packet of Marlboros. 'Take one, light it, and inhale,' he said. I immediately had a coughing fit, and Julie was sick in the bin. 'I haven't had a fag,' she protested, 'since I was fourteen.' Tim ignored her and prodded on the PowerPoint. Lines of text slid on and off. 'Smokers,' he said, 'change things. Smokers are clued up on office affairs, know what staff think of the company, are less risk averse and more alive to the moment. They're sensualists, pleasure-seekers and,' he snapped off the machine, 'never defer gratification. Smokers take action so from now on, the members of this management team are smokers. Tomorrow we'll look at lighting and holding, disposal of stubs, and when to offer and when to accept. And I have a few things to say about lunchtime drinking.'

Potato Smiles

WHEN DEBBIE LEFT I ate nothing but potato smiles with no-frills ketchup. One day I looked at the fluffy orange discs grinning up at me and decided to save one. I stuck it to the wall next to my bed and it cheered me up. The next day I saved another, but I'd had one of my funny days, so I stuck this one upside down, to make a frown. I did this for years and the pattern reminded me how well I was doing.

The man from environmental health had a big oblong body built for blocking doorways. 'The neighbours are talking about a smell,' he said.

I locked the door and made him sit while I removed the smiles and heaped them on a plate in front of him. The sauce bottle was rimmed with decaying ketchup scabs. I squeezed, squeezed hard till his plate was full.

Shop Talk

S HE DIDN'T WORK with people, she worked with structures. She talked their language, knew about business growth models, could joke about the inverted triangle of the not-for-profits, worked strategically, never operationally.

So why was she in bed with this ginger man, shagging a person not a structure, growing a relationship, not the growth model of a relationship, getting her hands dirty with service delivery?

I'd flown down to surprise her on her Managing Change course. And here she was. The woman who had written "Do Not Resuscitate" on a subordinate's personnel file, who shouted, 'Does the Pope have a wooden dick?' at the Regional Development Agency, who would rather grind monkeys than talk to organists.

Their heads touch on the pillow, his hog-orange bristles mingling with her chestnut locks. The contrasting shades remind me of exotic snakes, spiders as big as hands. It is the warning pattern of poison.

Until You are Happy

H E SAT IN the Photo-Me and read the instructions. *Tilt your head to the side or sit at an angle. Point your shoulder towards the camera.* He tried all this, but couldn't relax. He looked as though he was holding a contorted poise for an invasive medical examination. His face wore the expression of a startled comedian trying to look zany. Then he saw the sign. *Keep taking your picture until you are happy.* He stayed in the booth all day, striking a pose, taking the picture, looking at the preview screen, starting again. But each time the morose face staring back said the same thing. *There is no escape. There is no way out. You can get a travel card, but you'll never get away from me.*

Floydy

FRAGGLE-RALPH WON a competition: the Sugababes play live in your living room.

No-one had heard of the Sugababes and neither the word 'living' nor 'room' could describe our living space; sofa criss-crossed with masking tape, TV balanced on a toilet, a pyramid of Superstrengths in a shopping trolley.

Ralph sucked on his joint. 'Aren't they sort of, like, Floydy?'

Sugababes.com confirmed that the girls were not 'Floydy', nor would they be comfortable in a shabby house with two unemployed alcoholics and a bi-polar with anxiety episodes. But Fraggle-Ralph rang the number and you know the rest: street blocked with do-not-cross tape, counsellors crackling through loud-hailers, milk-faced publicist Sellotaped to a chair, and Fraggle-Ralph bawling, 'Sugababes now!' waving his .22 about.

At night the pigs blasted thrash-metal from a helicopter. Some of it sounded all right. The publicist kept crying, that was the problem. If she'd stopped crying everything would have been OK.

The Habits of Unstoppable People

'L ET'S WORK ON your narrative arc.' I looked blank so she took me to a party. It was all razor-edged suits, high-drain hairstyles, people who could slip in and out of social interactions like Porsche gear movements, who knew when to sip, nod, nibble, laugh, all to a background wash of clinking percussion and meandering oohs and aahs, like a music therapy class.

My mentor raced about, cheek-kissing and hand-pressing, between each blipvert tête-à-tête consulting a stopwatch on the underside of her wrist and muttering things like 'five seconds too long' or 'excellent closure.'

'Your narrative arc is your life,' she explained. 'If a relationship isn't pressing forward your personal narrative, cut it off. We are trapped in a narrative trajectory.' She described with her finger a tangled racetrack in the air. 'We cross, we mingle, but wait,' she glanced over my shoulder, 'someone's coming, act normal.'

The Way you Say 'Park'

H E HAD BEEN listening to her voice for years; the percussive, slightly guttural approach to Newton-le-Willows, the gorgeous ripe burr in the vowels of Hazel Grove, the absolute absence of sarcasm when she apologised for cancellations. Today he was singing along in his head as usual when he heard her inject a new enunciation into Eccelston Park, giving the word 'park' greater emphasis and putting a little suppressed laugh at the end of it.

This was significant because it was his name. Parker. And each time she said 'park' she made the same little flourish.

He decided not to go into work and instead stayed at the station, listening to the way she said 'park'. The staff wouldn't tell him where her office was, but tomorrow he would discover her name and shout it on all the platforms. That way she would know that he loved her in return.

Lady Pleaser

Darren was at the pub and Geraldine came round to keep me company.

'I saw your bloke today.' She winked at me, long and slow. 'That'll be keeping you smiling.'

'What?'

'The lady-pleaser!'

I laughed, pretending I understood. 'Oh, sure!'

When she'd gone I rang Steph. 'What's a lady-pleaser?'

'You mean in facial hair? It's a tuft of stubble under the bottom lip which, you know, enhances things when he goes south?'

Darren had recently grown a tiny jut-beard. 'Oh.'

When he goes south. Darren hadn't been

further than the Midlands with me for years.

When he got back from the pub the pathetic sprout of bristles bobbed up and down as the lies poured out, but I could see through him like a cheap nightie. She was some barmaid where he DJ'd. What upset me most was that she had to customise him, when for me he was always perfect.

First Out

THE ALARM EMITTED a vile digital shriek, the bed tilted and he climbed out. I rolled onto his side, now lovely and cool, and hoped for tea. Then I heard the computer bing-bong and the chatter of a keyboard. I slipped on my robe and crept downstairs. He was sat motionless in front of the screen on which an orangey-skinned woman in complicated underwear was being revealed. "Red hot amateurs" it said.

'Dougie,' I said. He didn't move. 'Do you always look at these sites?'

'I suppose.'

'Then what's this?' I hit enter and the screen filled up with platform numbers, times and destinations.

He began to quiver. 'I'm sorry darling, it's

just, ever since I stopped going in, I need to know about the trains. It gnaws away at me inside.'

I stroked his head. Outside the neighbour reversed his car into the thickening traffic.

Light Lunch

WE SAT AT a pavement table, the only customers brave enough for the September air.

'I warn you,' I told her, 'I have a chronic inability to attract the attention of waiters. So let's be nonchalant. Bury your head in the newspaper like you don't care, and your man in the apron will be straight over.'

After twenty minutes she frowned. 'Shouldn't this have worked by now?'

'Yeh. We'll move up a notch.' I popped over the road and brought back sandwiches. 'Start eating. They hate it when you do this.'

We left the newspapers and sandwich wrappers on the table. 'Never mind,' I said. 'We've had a cheap lunch and we're up to date with the news.'

When I returned, the waiter was on a fag break and he helped me return the table and chairs to my car. He had no idea what a fool this made him appear.

With Tongues

H E SAID HE was in the Albanian Builders Federation and I interpreted this for the immigration officer exactly, leaving out that the federation was nothing more than a drinking club for blokes with cement mixers. My job was to interpret, the rules were very strict. Then he said that the reason for his persecution was that he was gay. Now this immigration officer was a *Sun* reader who always mouthed off about homosexuals. So I had to change what he said from gay to a member of New-Free-Albania.

The officer wrote this down and looked at him. 'Who is the leader of New-Free-Albania?'

So I said in Albanian, 'Who is your favourite gay singer?'

He thought for a long time then said, in clear English, 'The Pet Shop Boys.'

I interpret for the police now and make things up all the time. It isn't a problem here, it actually helps.

On This Very Special Day

MY MOTHER LIVES in Cornwall and I always forget her birthday. So I bought a whole batch of cards, scribbled messages on them, and gave them to my sister who would drop one off each year. Average female life expectancy is seventy-nine, so I bought twenty-nine cards. It didn't seem a lot, but there it is.

Ten years later my sister said she wouldn't do it anymore. Watching the pile of cards getting smaller was depressing. Why couldn't I have bought like a hundred cards?

I hate waste so I tried my dad. 'There's not enough here,' he said. 'A woman in Japan lived to one hundred and twenty-six. I'll do it if you buy another fifty.'

I looked at him in disbelief.

'Those are my terms,' he said.

So I gave them to my mother who said it was fine and I believed her. After all, she brought me into the world.

Cica Lights

MUM AND TREVOR were getting serious, what with her new glittery top and the way she stroked the sleeve of his knobbly jumper like it was a hamster. But you can put up with that. When he bought me new trainers my heart sank. The box declared in scrolly italics, Clarks, and when I lifted the lid, pink lights winked through tissue and my worst fears were confirmed.

Cica Lights. A Nike copy with pathetic flashing bulbs in the heels.

I was dead if I wore them. Like the boy who wore a *Blue Peter* T-shirt on non-uniform day and had since developed a stutter and started hanging with the science-fiction lot.

So I told Trevor about the nights my dad stayed over and Trevor stormed out taking the shoes with him.

My mum was inconsolable. But relationships come and go. Your choice of trainer leaves an indelible mark.

The World Won't Listen

LUCY SCREECHED TO a halt, jumped out and stomped down the street. I sat for a time watching her diminishing figure in the mirror, then decided to catch her up. As I walked I noticed a sign in a shoe shop window: THIS IS NOT THE RAILWAY STATION and began to think about handmade signs. A lot of annoying things have to happen a lot of times to persuade you to make a sign. Company-made signs are obviously not good enough to communicate what the public need to know. They always have to get out their marker pens. Here was another, on a cake shop door: WE DO NOT SELL PIES.

I caught her up at McDonald's (NO ROLLER-BLADES) and followed her into the toilets where she sat down and cried in a cubicle. Blu Tacked above a murky mirror a sign said: THE TOILET BRUSH IS FOR STAFF USE ONLY.

Smack

MY TOLERANCE WAS down to one bar so I told this tosser where he could stick his complaint and Reg, who was call-monitoring, curled his finger at me to come over. He asked me to roll up my sleeve and then gripped my forearm in his hands and gave me a really hard Chinese-burn.

'Ow,' I said, more in surprise than anything else. The people around him carried on with their calls.

Later, when he heard me getting chatty with a female caller, he got out a plastic ruler and waited for me to offer my hand. 'Reg,' I said, 'no,' but he whacked me on the thigh.

From then on I ignored him. But the team-leader laid down the law. People like Reg paid the company a lot of money to come in and do

their thing and if I didn't like it I knew where
the off-switch was.

End of Line

I GOT THESE shoes from Aldi. Nine ninety-nine. Since the move to operations the quality of my appearance, which before was a pin in the hinge of my closing a contract, was not so vital.

But Andy wasn't happy. 'New shoes?'

I stuck out my foot and turned the heel. 'Yes.'

'Listen, I don't want to get all bottom-line but, those colours, it's like, Rover, your cornflakes are ready. Not very Waterson and Piper. You used to wear the sort of shoe that a pimp would lick.'

'I'm Operations now.'

'Still.'

'It's my doctor. She says I should wear bright things. For my health.'

I moved my desk in front of reception and sat with my feet up so all the visitors could see my shoes. Funny, but since I made up the stuff about bright colours it actually seemed to be working. I felt cheerful for the first time in ages.

Server Farmer

I T WAS THE three a.m. walk round and I had finished checking the data feeds when I looked back at the servers squatting in the dim aquarium light. They seemed to be mocking me with their beady glittering eyes. These Daleks belonged to all kinds of companies – a nuclear plant, the Benefit Agency, a vehicle breakdown company. I imagined them swapping stories when I'd gone – about caesium spills, dodgy claims, flat batteries in howling gales. I knew for certain that they talked about me.

A spangled map showed the live server connections and when I flipped the switches a thousand winking stars went out. I sensed a body go limp, thought I heard a sigh as the last breath of data escaped. Sirens howled, lights flashed, Doc Marten'd feet pounded down the corridor.

I knew what it was like to kill and I had to have more.

Kick inside

M

Y GP WAS sceptical, but I insisted, you have to nowadays, and a week later the consultant was inserting a tube with a camera on the end into my bowel. Pink folds of glistening skin moved past like rippling sand. 'That's normal tissue,' he said. 'but I'll explore further.' The screen went dark then there she was, Sheila, my dead wife, pressing a panel of buttons on a small control box, a faint smile on her face. She knew we could see her, knew that the snaking black tube was capturing her image.

'I see,' the consultant said.

'She's been there for months,' I told him. 'She controls me. She makes me eat Battenburg cake.'

There's no treatment apparently. But they

gave me a print-out of the screen. That's it on the fridge door. She's making me tell you this, I wasn't going to bother.

Pop-Tarts

THE LANDLORD WAS known as 'Pop-Tarts' and for some reason this worried me. I asked him right away about Deborah and he laughed and shook his large bulbous head.

'Deborah? Which story did she spin you?' Something went *Ker-ching!* and I followed his eyes to a row of mahogany-coloured rectangles poking out of a monstrous aluminium toaster.

'She was only fifteen,' I told him.

'They come and go. Transients. See that?' Grey sheets of smoke billowed out of the gleaming toaster. 'Proof I do breakfast. Means I get to be a boarding house, do the homeless.' He chuckled, showing stumpy brown teeth. 'There's money in street people.'

'Was Debbie . . .'

'She was different. It's mainly druggies and alchies come through here. Where is the noble tramp, the gentleman of the road?' He flipped the scorched pastries onto a plate and incandescent red globules oozed out. 'Who'd have kids, eh?'

The Funny Way I Feel Inside

I RESTED MY forehead against the cold chromium rail in front so I could hear what the cute pixie girl was saying.

'I could never go out with a boy who didn't love, love, love the sound of rain,' she told her mate. 'That's a real deal-breaker for me.'

Later that week it was really hammering down so I followed her into a bus-shelter. I threw my head back and closed my eyes. I stretched my fingers like a pianist. I hummed and rolled my head from side to side.

But when I opened my eyes she'd gone.

I stayed there listening to the pulsing of the drops. If there was ever an overrated sound, it's the sound of rain. It's not even actually the sound of rain. Rain itself doesn't make a sound. What you hear is a much more complex phenomenon, more intricate than she could ever imagine.

The Heartless Chain

SOMEONE SUCKED THE soul out of Palouki's bar. We'd gone back there to rekindle the love in our marriage, but Helen wasn't impressed, believing the place had been gobbled up by some heartless chain. I deduced that old Palouki had passed it on to his son. I knew I was right, as was usually the case, but I didn't push it; the job was to rekindle.

When our food arrived a photographer appeared and asked if he could take some pictures for outside the restaurant. Helen laughed girlishly, threw her arms about me and waited for the flash.

But the photographer was focussing on our plate of meze.

'The pictures fade fast,' he explained. 'Since

the old man retired, his son wants everything so-so.'

I winked at Helen, but she began to cry. Just imagine it. Our special dinner, outside for all to see. How many people can say that?'

The Man Whose Head Expanded

I MAGINE YOUR MIND has left your body and is hovering in front of you. Can you see it? A clump of steam, straining on the end of a silver thread? Feels OK, doesn't it? But soon the thread will snap and it will float away. Hopefully you'll have thought ahead and closed the window tight, but it will bat against the walls like a trapped bluebottle, trying to escape.

Ask it what it wants.

It will say, 'To be free. To go where the other minds live.'

Open the window and follow it.

That's how I got here. It's a bit dull, actually. Sometimes I'm allowed to float outside on a silver string, but usually I just keep things tidy, and maintain the diary of appointments.

Practical stuff really, grunt work, whilst my mind thinks long clear unbroken thoughts that go on forever, something it longed to do for years.

A Personal Message

I T BOILED DOWN to a fear of novelty ceramic objects, that's all, but this doctor fellah took it very seriously.

He clasped his hands together. 'Your, er, system. Is it closed or open?'

'System?' I thought for a bit. 'I'm very open.'

He glanced down at his papers. 'Then you need a key. To release the pressure.'

'But where is the key?'

'You have the key. It comes with the system.'

The central heating droned and hiccupped and he looked at the radiator.

'Sometimes,' he added, 'there's a build-up of thick sludge.' He sighed. 'Complete draining is required.'

I snatched the papers from his hand. It was the instruction manual for the boiler. I looked at it and smiled. Tomorrow I would collect all the instruction manuals from around my house. It was as I suspected. Every piece of printed material ever produced contained a personal message for me.

Doctor Logic

IT TURNED OUT that the lads had an insulting nickname for every manager apart from me, and according to the gurus, this is a sign of enormous affection, so I had to get one too.

I tried everything. An elaborate corkscrewing limp, a breathy *ee-aw* sound when I spoke, but nothing happened.

'I'm at a crossroads,' I explained to Gary. 'One way I get a nickname, the other way, oblivion. Could you arrange for me to be called a funny name?'

'That's not a crossroads,' Gary said. 'That's a T-junction.'

After he'd gone I thought about how logical he was. I rang Keith.

'Keith, I've been talking to Doctor Logic.'

'Who the fuck is Doctor Logic?'

'Gary. You know how he's always logical.'

Soon everyone would be saying Doctor Logic and when Gary discovered the favour I'd done him, I was sure he would devise a suitable name for me.

Dead Star

I WAS OFF sick from the buses with my back when I saw the ad for a park-keeper and I thought what the hell? I'm stuck here, drowning in afternoon telly pap, why shouldn't I do something useful? So I got a start with parks and after a week of trowelling rang in sick on that job too. That's when it struck me; there's no limit to the jobs you can be off sick from. I bought an *Evening News*, got four more jobs and after a few weeks called in sick to all of them.

Keeping it up was a full time occupation. There were six Christmas dos. Yet I was addicted. I conjured with multiple homes, multiple wives, a thousand parallel existences, each nourishing the other. Because somewhere in the universe I was already gone; a star that burns in our sky but died a million years ago.

Think About it Baby

THIS IS NOT about the money. It's about the gorgeous curved stem of the headset and the cute bobble microphone. It's not just till something better comes along. It's about the giant slabs of data shuddering into life at my command, the cooing sing-song script, the juicy clack-clack of the keyboards, the whispering disembodied voices at three a.m..

But my accent wasn't right. They'd set up in Middlesbrough for the lovely Geordie lilt and I hailed from Swindon.

Viz is on the top shelf and I can see why. It took three months of reading aloud, but before long I'd nailed it and was back in the nest.

It was even better. They loved my voice. Would I say something else? Would I repeat a word? Did I know how sexy I sounded?

Tony from Crawley wanted to marry me and I think I might take up his offer.

Life Just Bounces

THE SALESMAN'S SKIN glistened with sweat. 'Where's the big money?' he cried.

'Bouncy castles!' we replied.

'Correctamundo!' His legs quivered like a manic preacher's. 'And I know that those of you who respect yourselves as people will sign up today.'

The words of the presentation echoed in my head as I stared at the rusted generator and sagging vinyl edifice that covered the lawn. All my redundancy, everything, sunk into this. Rowena would kill me. I had no van to transport it and no money for advertising.

I switched on the power, the generator throbbed and clunked, and slowly the gaudy plastic puddle rose up to become a quivering enchanted fairy palace. I thought about the others back at work, the ones who had been kept on. Then I flicked off my shoes and jumped in. I bounced. It was good, bouncing away. The salesman was right. Everybody wants to bounce.